Cinderella

RETOLD FROM THE BROTHERS GRIMM
AND ILLUSTRATED BY NONNY HOGROGIAN
GREENWILLOW BOOKS • NEW YORK

Library of Congress Cataloging in Publication Data: Hogrogian, Nonny. Cinderella. Summary: In her haste to flee the palace before the fairy godmother's magic loses effect, Cinderella leaves behind a glass slipper. [1. Fairy tales. 2. Folklore—Germany] I. Grimm, Jakob Ludwig Karl, 1785-1863. Aschenputtel. II. Title. PZ8.H687Ci 398.2'2'0943 [E] 80-15394 ISBN 0-688-80299-0 ISBN 0-688-84299-2 (lib. bdg.)

FOR OUR CHILDREN

Once upon a time there lived a nobleman and his wife and their beautiful young daughter. The wife had been ill for a long time and when she knew she was dying, she called her daughter to her bedside.

"My dear child," she said, "always be as good as you are now and I promise you will be protected. Although I cannot be here at your side as you grow, I will be watching over you." With these words she closed her eyes and died.

The maiden went to her mother's grave every day and wept. When winter came, the snow spread a blanket over the grave, but when the sun of springtime uncovered it again, the nobleman found a new wife.

The stepmother arrived with her own two daughters, who were beautiful to look at but cold and cruel inside. They could not stand the fact that their young stepsister not only was beautiful but was good at heart as well.

"We will not allow this stupid goose in the parlor with us," they cried. "She's nothing better than a kitchen maid. If she wants bread, she must earn it."

And with that they barred her from the parlor and their family life, such as it was. They took away her beautiful clothes and left her some rags to wear and a pair of old wooden clogs.

They gave her chores to do from morning until late at night. She lit the fires at dawn and scrubbed the house and cooked their meals and carried in the water and washed their clothes. At night she didn't even have a pillow to rest her head on, but slept on the hearth among the cinders and the ashes. And so they began to call her Cinderella.

The sisters constantly abused her with scorn and insults and they teased her and even shook bags of peas into the ashes to make her pick them out again.

One day Cinderella's father prepared to go on a journey, and asked the sisters what they would like him to bring them. One asked for dresses and the other for jewels.

"And you, Cinderella? What shall I bring for you?"

"Oh, Papa," she answered, "I would like a fresh green hazel twig, the first one you brush against on your way home."

And so the nobleman bought elegant gowns and rich jewels for the two older girls. He took care of various other matters and started back. As he was riding along a narrow path, a small green hazel twig brushed his hat and knocked it off his head. "How fortunate for the reminder," he thought, and picking up his hat he snapped off the little twig and rode on.

The stepsisters were delighted with their gowns and jewels, and paraded in front of their mirrors in all their vanity.

Cinderella thanked her father for the hazel twig and went out and planted it on her mother's grave. She wept so much that her tears watered the shoot, and before very long it grew into a beautiful hazel tree. Each day a small white dove flew into the tree, and if Cinderella had a wish, there would be a rustling in the tree, and suddenly her wish would be granted.

When some time had passed, the King proclaimed a festival which was to last three days and three nights. He invited all the young ladies of the kingdom so that his son might choose a bride.

When the two stepsisters heard the news, they were full of hope and excitement, and they ordered Cinderella about more than ever. Cinderella obeyed their orders, but she, too, wished to go to the ball.

"You, Cinderella?" cried the stepmother. "You are covered with ashes and you haven't a thing to wear. How can you possibly go to the ball?"

But as Cinderella again urged her stepmother to let her go, the stepmother decided to teach her a lesson. "Very well," she said, and she tossed a tubful of peas into the cinders. "If you can pick out all the good ones in one hour, then you may go to the ball with us."

Cinderella knew that she could not possibly get the task done by herself, but she also knew that her hazel tree was a magical tree and was the home of the fairy dove. She went out to the hazel tree and told the dove about the peas in the ashes. No sooner had she spoken, than a flock of birds flew into the house, and peck, peck, peck, they gathered all the good peas into the tub and flew out again.

Cinderella took the tub to her stepmother, only to be told once more that she couldn't go to the ball because she had no proper clothes and they would be ashamed of her. With this she turned her back on Cinderella and left the room.

When her stepmother and stepsisters left for the ball, Cinderella wasted no time. She scrubbed herself, brushed her hair and went out to the hazel tree. There was a rustling in the branches, and in a moment Cinderella's rags turned into a gown that seemed to be made of the stars in the sky, and in place of wooden shoes, she was wearing silver slippers.

Then a soft voice whispered, "Be home before midnight." And a fine carriage pulled by six white horses appeared with a coachman and footman in blue and silver livery.

When Cinderella arrived at the ball, she looked so beautiful and radiant that even her stepmother and stepsisters didn't recognize her. The Prince asked her to be his partner and they danced and danced while all the guests wondered where this great beauty had come from.

As the clock struck quarter to twelve, Cinderella slipped away and the Prince had no idea what had happened to her.

When the stepmother and stepsisters arrived home, they found Cinderella lying among the ashes in her old rags.

The next day, as soon as they had gone, Cinderella again went out to the hazel tree.

There was a rustle and a shake and suddenly Cinderella looked more beautiful than the evening before. Her gown was made completely of pearls, and on her feet were delicately embroidered slippers to match.

The Prince had been waiting for her. He took her hand and would dance with no one else. But once again, as the clock struck a quarter to midnight, Cinderella rushed away. And again when the family returned home, she appeared to be sleeping among the ashes.

On the third day Cinderella dressed the two sisters with even more care than before, while they gossiped about the mysterious maiden at the ball.

As soon as their carriage drove away, she ran to the hazel tree. The dove cooed down to her. There was a rustling in the branches and Cinderella was transformed.

This time she looked like sunlight itself, her golden hair cascading over a gown of pure gold, and on her feet were two golden slippers.

The Prince never left Cinderella's side, and so in love was she with the prince that she forgot about time.

Suddenly she heard the first stroke of midnight and she fled the ball.

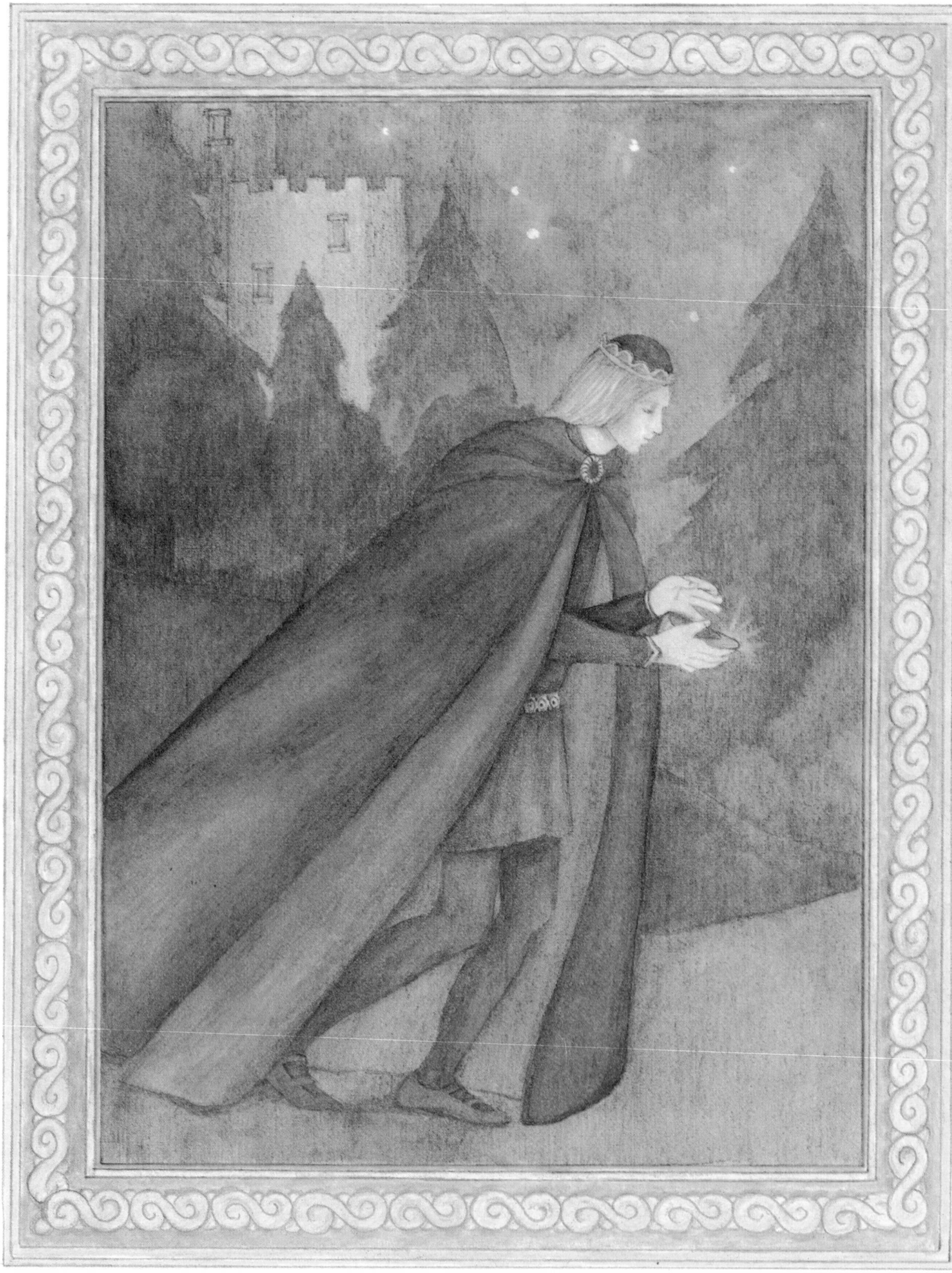

The Prince tried to follow her, but she was out of the palace grounds and gone before he knew it. As he turned to go back, he noticed a golden slipper shining in the grass. He carefully picked it up and carried it to the palace.

When Cinderella reached home, she was in her rags again and all that remained of her finery was the golden slipper which she had removed when its mate had slipped from her foot.

The next day the Prince announced that he would marry the maiden whose foot the golden slipper fit. There were many who tried to wear the slipper, but to no avail. There were duchesses and princesses and all the ladies of the court, but the slipper was either too wide or too narrow, too long or too short, and not one of them had a foot that was just right for the golden slipper.

Finally, the Prince himself went from house to house, looking for the rightful owner of the slipper.

Cinderella's stepsisters were very excited for they both had beautiful feet. When the Prince arrived at their house, the elder sister took the slipper to her room to try it on. Her mother watched eagerly, but the girl could not get her foot into the slipper. Her big toe was too large. Her mother brought her a knife, saying, "Cut off a piece of your toe; if you become Queen you will no longer need to go by foot." So the girl cut off a piece of her toe and squeezed her foot into the slipper. When the Prince saw the slipper on her foot, he thought she must be the mysterious maiden. He lifted her onto his horse and started for the palace.

As they passed the hazel tree, the small white dove flew along beside him, and as the Prince turned to look at the bird, he noticed blood trickling out of the slipper. He realized the girl had lied and took her home.

The younger sister took the slipper to her room to try it on. Her toes slipped in easily but her heel was too wide. The mother, reaching for the knife, again said, "Cut a piece off your heel. When you are Queen, you will not need to do any walking." So the younger stepsister cut a piece off her heel and managed to get her foot into the slipper. She hid her pain and went down to the Prince. He placed her on his horse, and once again he started for his palace. And once again the dove flew along beside him. The Prince turned and saw blood dripping on the ground and he knew this maiden, too, had tricked him.

He took her home, and asked the nobleman, "Have you no other daughter?" The father replied, "Cinderella is my daughter, but she could not possibly be the bride you seek."

"I wish to see her," said the Prince.

"No!" cried the stepmother. "She is much too ragged and dirty to present herself to a prince."

But the Prince would have his way and Cinderella was summoned. She scrubbed her face and brushed the ashes from her hair. As she entered the room, she bowed deeply before the Prince, then offered her delicate foot. It slipped easily into the golden slipper, and taking its mate out of her pocket she slipped it on her other foot. As she stood up and raised her head, the Prince recognized the beautiful maiden of the ball.

"How could I have been so mistaken?" he cried. "Cinderella is my bride!"

The stepsisters turned white with rage, but the Prince carried Cinderella to his horse and rode away. As they passed the hazel tree, the little white dove flew down and nestled on Cinderella's shoulder.

The marriage was celebrated with great festivities and the two stepsisters were stricken blind as a punishment for their wickedness.

- 3/86

4/8/86 ✓

DATE			

© THE BAKER & TAYLOR CO.